Lucky, Lucky White Horse

by Beryl Epstein

Pictures by Mia Carpenter

Lucky, Lucky White Horse

Harper & Row, Publishers
New York, Evanston, and London

Contents

Lucky, Lucky White Horse

Chapter 1 ✳ *Moving Day*

Ellen dried the last cup and reached up to hang it in the cupboard.

Aunt Jo emptied the dishpan. "There!" she said. "That's done!"

It was almost five o'clock on moving day. Ellen Evans and her mother and father and the baby had left their old home in Marysville early that morning. The furniture had gone to Columbus ahead of them, in two big moving wagons. It was waiting when they reached the two-family house on Summit Street.

Aunt Jo had been waiting for them too, to help them get settled. She had moved to Columbus the year before, when she started teaching school.

Now the rugs were laid. The furniture was in place. The curtains were hung. Mrs. Evans was making up the beds. And Aunt Jo and Ellen had just unpacked and washed all the everyday dishes.

Aunt Jo untied her apron. "Let's go cool off on the porch," she said. "I think we deserve a rest."

Ellen stopped at the foot of the stairs in the living room. "Mother!" she called softly. The baby was already asleep. She didn't want to wake him. "We're going out on the porch."

"I'll join you in a few minutes," her mother whispered back. Ellen leaned against the railing that separated the two porches of the house. Her cousin Hetty's family would move into the other half of the house in three weeks.

Aunt Jo fanned herself with her handkerchief. "Are you excited, Ellen?" she asked. "Do you think you'll look back, when you're grown up, and say 1916 was the most important year of your life?"

"Because we moved to Columbus, you mean?" Ellen asked.

Aunt Jo nodded. She sat down on the top step. Ellen sat beside her.

"Maybe," Ellen said. She knew she would be more

excited if Hetty weren't going to live next door. But she was afraid Aunt Jo wouldn't understand if she said so.

"Why 'maybe'?" Aunt Jo asked.

"Well," Ellen said, "if it were just our family here, then—"

She stopped. She couldn't say, Then I could be my real self for once. All my life Hetty has treated me like her shadow. So that's what everybody in Marysville thinks I am. But in Columbus nobody knows me. So I could be different here. I'm sure I could! But if Hetty's here too, it will go on being just the same.

"I know, dear," Aunt Jo said. "You're lonely now, by yourself. But in just three weeks you and Hetty will be together again, the way you've always been."

"Yes," Ellen said in a small voice. She knew nobody would ever understand, not even Aunt Jo who understood most things. "In three weeks it will be just like always."

She was afraid she was going to cry. Her throat felt funny. Tears came into her eyes. She blinked fast and pretended to be looking out at Summit Street.

A trolley was clanging past. Behind it came one of the new automobiles. Hetty had said there would probably be at least twenty automobiles in a city as big as Columbus.

A grocery wagon rattled by in the opposite direction.

"What a lot there is to watch on Summit Street!" Aunt Jo said. "Why, goodness me! There's a white horse!"

And suddenly Aunt Jo gave a lick to her right thumb, like a man getting ready to fight.

"Lucky, lucky white horse!" she said. Then she struck her right fist into her left palm three times. "Ding! Ding! Ding!" she said. There was a Ding! for each blow.

Ellen stared at her.

"What's the matter?" Aunt Jo asked. "Don't you count white horses? And say 'Lucky, lucky white horse! Ding! Ding! Ding!' every time you see one?"

Ellen shook her head.

"Now imagine that!" Aunt Jo said. "I thought everybody counted white horses."

"But why do they?" Ellen asked.

"Because when you have counted a hundred white horses," Aunt Jo said, "and walk around the block— straight around, without stopping—you're supposed to find something."

"I never knew that!" Ellen said. She was pretty sure Hetty didn't either. "Does it work?" she asked.

Aunt Jo laughed. "To tell the truth, Ellen," she said, "I don't know. I never got all the way to a hundred myself.

I keep starting. But then I forget where I am and have to start over. I've heard of it working for other people, though. At least I think I have."

The screen door opened. Ellen's mother came out.

Ellen and Aunt Jo moved apart, to make room for her between them.

"Poor Nell!" Aunt Jo said. "You look tired out."

"I guess we're all tired," Mrs. Evans said. "It seems months ago that we left Marysville. Doesn't it, Ellen?"

Ellen nodded. But she wasn't really thinking about leaving Marysville that morning. She was thinking what fun it would be, for once, to tell Hetty something she didn't know.

"Guess what?" Ellen would say, the very day Hetty moved in. "Did you know that if you count a hundred white horses and then walk straight around the block, without stopping, you're supposed to find something?"

Hetty was sure to be surprised. Maybe even impressed.

Upstairs the baby began to cry. Mrs. Evans sighed and got up and went back into the house.

An ice wagon was coming along. The horse drawing it was white.

"There's another one, Aunt Jo!" Ellen said. "Quick! Show me what you do!"

Aunt Jo licked her right thumb. Ellen licked hers too.

"Lucky, lucky white horse!" Aunt Jo said.

"Lucky, lucky white horse!" Ellen said.

"Ding! Ding! Ding!" Aunt Jo struck her right fist into her left palm each time she said Ding!

"Ding! Ding! Ding!" Ellen said and hit her left palm with her right fist at each word.

Aunt Jo laughed and hugged her. "Good for you! Now you have horse number one! You'll probably get to a hundred in no time here. Because if that same wagon comes by tomorrow, you can count the horse again. So with just that one wagon, you see, you'd have thirty horses in a month."

She stood up. "Now I'd better go in and put some supper on the table. Your father should be along soon."

Alone on the porch, Ellen began to think hard. "If I counted four horses every day," she thought, "I'd have a hundred in just twenty-five days! Or if I counted five in a day, I'd have a hundred in only—in only twenty days!"

It was exciting to think of walking around the block, in just twenty days, and maybe finding something.

Then Ellen thought. "But in twenty days Hetty won't even be here!"

Suddenly all the excitement was gone.

"I'll have to wait until she comes," Ellen told herself. "She wouldn't like it if I didn't."

Ellen stood up and looked across the railing at the porch that would be Hetty's porch in three weeks. She could imagine Hetty there, on the day they both counted their last white horse. By then Hetty would have decided just what they should do.

"You take one side of the walk, Ellen," Hetty would probably say. "I'll take the other. No fair peeking ahead. And if you happen to see something on my side, it will belong to me. Because we'll each have our own side. Do you understand?"

That's how it would be, Ellen knew. Hetty would give orders, and she would expect Ellen to obey.

Ellen glared at the empty porch next door. "It would serve you right," she said, "if I didn't wait for you at all!"

There was nobody on the porch to answer her.

"It would serve you right!" Ellen repeated.

And that very instant she made up her mind.

She wasn't going to wait for Hetty.

"I have already counted one horse," she said out loud. Her voice was very firm. "So I am just going to keep going. And when I get to a hundred, I'll walk around the block all by myself. And whatever I find will belong to me. And I will find something. I just know I will!"

Ellen felt excited all over again. A lot more excited than before. She sat on the broad flat top of the railing, swung her feet up, and hugged her knees.

What would she find? she wondered.

A penny, perhaps, that someone had dropped? Or even a dime?

Or maybe a lost ring with a stone in it? Or a silver pin? Or a locket?

Ellen giggled. "Don't be silly!" she told herself. "How could you ever find anything like that? Anyway it won't matter what you find, so long as you just find something."

That was when she knew.

It was like suddenly knowing that if you didn't step on a single crack all the way home from school, there'd be chocolate cake for supper.

Ellen *knew* that if she found something when she walked around the block, it would make everything different. Whatever she found would be magic. No matter what it was, even an old nail. It would be a magic charm that would transform her into somebody who would never be Hetty's shadow again.

It really would.

Ellen shut her eyes. "I just know it would!" she whispered.

And when she opened her eyes there was a white horse pulling a vegetable wagon right past the house.

That proved it, Ellen thought. It was going to work!

Swiftly she licked her thumb. "Lucky, lucky white horse!" she said. "Ding! Ding! Ding!"

Chapter 2 ✳ *The House on the Corner*

When Ellen woke up in the morning she pushed back the covers and jumped out of bed. The house was quiet. Nobody else was awake.

She got dressed and tiptoed down the stairs.

At the porch door she stopped. She didn't want to answer questions about what she was doing outdoors so early. But she didn't want to waste any time.

She thought for a moment. Then she decided to set the table. Anybody who saw her doing that wouldn't guess that she was really watching for white horses through the dining room window.

Carefully she laid the cloth. Two trolleys went by.

She got out the plates. A wagon passed with a team of grays.

Ellen was counting out silver when she saw the white horse pulling a dairy cart. She almost dropped the spoons.

"Lucky, lucky white horse!" she said quickly. "Ding! Ding! Ding!"

But there hadn't been any need to hurry. The dairy cart stopped in front of the Evans house.

A man in white overalls started toward the back door. Milk bottles rattled in his metal basket.

Ellen opened the door. "Good morning," she said.

"Good morning to you! You're up early! I'm your milkman," the man said. "Welcome to Summit Street." He handed her two bottles.

"Thank you," Ellen said. "You have a nice horse."

"That's Whitey," he told her. "He knows my route better than I do. Tomorrow he'll stop here without being told."

"You mean Whitey will come here every morning?"

"Rain or shine!" the milkman said.

"That's wonderful!" Ellen smiled. "Then I'll look for you again tomorrow."

"And Whitey and I will look for you, miss." The milkman tipped his cap as he left, as if she were the lady of the house.

Mrs. Evans came downstairs a few minutes later. She looked at the table, ready for breakfast. Then she saw Ellen. "What a lovely surprise!" she said.

Ellen hugged her good morning. "I'm going to do it every day," she said.

Mrs. Evans raised one eyebrow. She was smiling. "I won't hold you to that," she said. "I know how much you like to sleep late on summer mornings."

"You'll see," Ellen said.

"All right." Mrs. Evans hugged her back. "We'll both see. And now let's eat together, just the two of us. The way we used to do before George was born."

"Oh, Mother! Let's!" Ellen said.

Mrs. Evans made Ellen's favorite, French toast. It was a wonderful breakfast.

Mr. Evans smiled when he joined them. "You're a sight to start a man's day off right," he said, kissing them both.

"Ellen had the table all set when I came down," Mrs. Evans told him.

"She did! Well, I just wish I knew a boy with as much get-up-and-go as that," Mr. Evans said. "I could certainly use his help in the store, at least until John comes."

John was Hetty's father. He and Mr. Evans owned a hardware store in Marysville. Now they were opening one in Columbus.

"It's a shame John isn't here now," Mrs. Evans said. "I'm sure you're working too hard."

"It can't be helped," Mr. Evans said. "John has his hands full too, training the new Marysville manager."

A hungry howl sounded from upstairs.

"Oh, dear!" Mrs. Evans looked at Ellen. "There's the end of our peace and quiet for today. And with so much still to do to get the house really settled!"

"I could take him out for the whole morning," Ellen said.

For the second time that day her mother raised an eyebrow. Ellen knew why. Taking George out in his carriage was the thing Ellen always hated most to do.

But taking him out now would be a good way to watch for white horses.

"I wouldn't mind, Mother," Ellen said. "There's so much to look at around here."

"Then bless you, Ellen!" Mrs. Evans said. "With George off my hands until his feeding time, I might even be able to make a chocolate cake for supper."

George looked pink and white and handsome in his carriage. He was almost asleep. Ellen tried not to joggle him awake.

She looked up and down the street, deciding where to go. She didn't want to walk around the block. She wanted to save that for the day she counted her one-hundredth white horse.

"I'll go as far as the corner and take a look down that side street," she decided.

She walked slowly. A trolley went past every few minutes. She saw two automobiles at almost the same time. And there were wagons of all kinds. But every horse was gray or brown or dappled. Not one of them was white.

Near the corner she found herself beside a tall iron

fence. Inside it was a smooth green lawn, with trees and neat flower beds, and a red brick house. It was the biggest house on the street. And it had a tower rising above its roof on one side.

"Like a castle!" Ellen said to herself.

She followed the fence around the corner, still staring at the big house. She wondered what sort of people lived in it.

Suddenly something moved behind one of the windows in the tower. Ellen stopped and squinted up at it.

George began to cry.

"Shh!" Ellen whispered. "Look, George! Just look!" Sometimes she could make him stop crying by talking to him. "There! Did you see? It was a girl—and she waved to us!"

Ellen raised her hand and waved back.

Then she said, "Oh!" Because the girl had disappeared. Now there was an old woman at the window in her place. Thin hands pushed the window up. A thin face peered down at Ellen.

"Don't stand there staring, little girl!" the old woman called. "Go away!"

Ellen's hands gripped the carriage bar. She was too frightened to move.

"Go away!" the woman called again, in a shrill angry voice. "Scat! Go on! Run!"

Ellen made herself give the carriage a hard push. George yelled. He kept on yelling.

Ellen didn't even hear him. Her heart was pounding. She was running as fast as she could go.

"Whoa, there! Whoa! Where's the fire, young lady?" A man in a blue uniform jumped up from a chair at the edge of the sidewalk. He stood right in front of the carriage.

Ellen had to stop.

"That's better!" The man smiled. "I'm the fireman around here," he told her. "Cap'n Zollinger's my name. You running to a fire, you'd better tell me about it."

Ellen swallowed. "No," she said. "It's not a fire. I was just— Oh, George! Shush!"

"Tell you what," Captain Zollinger said. "I'll show George something to cheer him up. In here."

Beside the chair he had been sitting in, the firehouse door was wide open. Captain Zollinger pushed the carriage toward it.

Ellen followed. Her heart wasn't beating quite so fast now. But she was still breathing hard, and her throat was dry.

Inside the firehouse, near the right wall, stood a shiny red fire engine. On the other side were two horse stalls. And the horses in them were white—both of them! They were white as snow.

"There now!" Captain Zollinger was saying. "What do you think of Bess and Betsy, George?"

Behind his back Ellen licked her right thumb and hit her left palm three times with her fist. "Lucky, lucky white horse! Ding! Ding! Ding!" she said under her breath.

Then she did the same thing again. "That's five!" she said.

The fireman was showing George the fire engine. George's fat hand reached toward it. His baby face was one big smile.

Captain Zollinger turned toward Ellen.

"Now what was all this running about, young lady?" he asked. "There's nothing to run away from in this neighborhood."

Before she knew it, Ellen was telling him about the girl and about the old woman. "Nobody ever chased me before!" she said. Even remembering it made her voice shake.

"That was Mrs. Ogilvie," the fireman said. "Ogre Ogilvie, my grandson called her one time when she chased him."

"Does she chase everybody?" Ellen asked.

"She don't like folks staring at the house," the captain said. "And lots of folks have been doing that since the tragedy. They even come up Summit Street on the trolleys, just to stare."

"What was the—tragedy?" Ellen asked.

"Her son and his wife and daughter were killed in an accident," Captain Zollinger said. "Happened about three months back. In one of those new automobiles. Terrible thing! All three alive one minute—and dead the next! The news of it just about killed Mrs. Ogilvie too."

"How awful!" Ellen said. Then her hand flew to her mouth. "But the girl I waved to—was she a ghost?"

"Fiddlesticks! You were waving to Mindy," the captain said. "It was her mamma and papa and sister that died."

"How awful!" Ellen said again.

"It is that," the captain agreed. "Mindy lives with her grandma now, of course. And the poor woman keeps her shut up as if she thought the sun would melt her. I guess she's afraid something will happen to Mindy too, and a body can understand how she feels. But folks shouldn't live like that, to my way of thinking."

He had been looking very sober as he talked. Now sud-

denly he smiled. "Here comes that scalawag grandson of mine," he said. Even his voice had changed.

A red-haired boy, a few years older than Ellen, was

swinging down the street. He was whistling.

"Jim plays checkers with me these days," Captain Zollinger said. "He wanted to work this summer, but there weren't any jobs lying about. So he keeps me company instead."

"Thank you very much for showing us your horses," Ellen said quickly. "And your fire engine." She was turning the carriage around. Hetty always knew what to say to boys. Ellen never did. "We'll have to go now."

"Come back any time," Captain Zollinger said. "Firehouse is open every day of the week."

"Thank you." Ellen was already several steps away. "Good-by."

"Good-by," Captain Zollinger said. "And you just wave a hand at that tower window when you go by Mrs. Ogilvie's," he added. "If Mindy sees you, it would cheer her up."

Ellen didn't answer. Perhaps he would think she hadn't heard. She was sure she wouldn't dare to wave. She hated even having to walk back past the big red brick house.

But when she came to it she did look up at the tower. Just once, very quickly. No one was standing at any of its windows.

"There's no point in waving if she can't see me," Ellen told George.

Then she knew she couldn't be sure whether Mindy would see her or not.

Suddenly she raised her head and smiled straight at the empty windows. At the same time she lifted her hand in a swift wave.

George made a happy noise, like oatmeal beginning to boil. Ellen smiled at the top of his head.

"That wasn't hard after all," she told him. "I could do that every day, I guess." She was pushing the carriage steadily toward the corner of Summit Street. "I could do it just as easy as not."

Chapter 3 ✳ *Checkers and Gumdrops*

Ellen sat on the porch that night, waiting for her father. The delicious smell of chocolate cake was coming from the kitchen. She had just counted her sixth horse for the day. With the two from the night before, she had eight altogether.

She saw Mr. Evans coming toward the house. He walked slowly, as if he were tired.

Suddenly two ideas came together in Ellen's head.

One idea was that her father needed help at the store.

The other idea was that Captain Zollinger's grandson, Jim, wanted a job.

"My goodness!" Ellen said, and jumped up and ran to meet her father.

He listened to her. Then he smiled. "I'll go around past the firehouse first thing in the morning," he said. "And we shall see what we shall see."

The next evening, on the very same spot, he told her it was settled.

"Jim is glad to have a job," he said. "And I'm glad to have him. And we both owe it all to a certain smart young lady." He took Ellen's hand and put it through his arm. It was the way he walked with her mother sometimes.

Ellen felt as if she were floating along above the sidewalk.

"There's just one problem," Mr. Evans said. "Captain Zollinger will miss his checker games. So he wants you to play with him. You could bring George, he says."

"I know." Ellen smiled. "I saw him this morning too."

She had walked past the firehouse to count Bess and Betsy. With Whitey, the milkman's horse, and three more she had seen from the porch in the afternoon, she had fourteen now.

"Did you say you would?" her father asked.

Ellen nodded.

"Good. But I've warned him," Mr. Evans said. "I told

him you were pretty hard to beat."

"Oh, Daddy!" Ellen said. "That's not true." But she felt very pleased.

The next day was Sunday. Summit Street was quiet and almost empty. But the milkman came as usual. And she saw the fire horses, even though the captain's assistant was on duty. So she had seventeen now. She was sure she would easily get to a hundred before Hetty arrived.

"Jim wants me to thank you," Captain Zollinger said on Monday morning. "He sent you these. Bought out of his first day's pay." He handed Ellen a paper sack.

Ellen could feel her face getting red. She bent it over the bag. "Gumdrops!" she said. "They're my favorites!"

"Glad to know it," the captain said. "I'll keep some on hand from now on. Loser gets one. Winner gets two."

He had the checkerboard already set up. They played until Ellen had to take George home for his eleven o'clock feeding. They each won three games.

The next morning they played again. And the morning after that.

Once Jim stopped by on his way to do an errand for her father. He stood behind Ellen's chair. When she didn't notice that she could take the captain's king, he showed her.

"Go along. Get back to work," the captain said. "I've enough trouble beating her without you helping out."

Jim winked at Ellen and left.

Ellen thought he must be a good player. She wondered if he'd ask her to play with him sometime. But of course the captain was fun to play with too. She made up her mind to win all the rest of the games that day. She almost did. She lost only one.

When she went to bed Wednesday night she had been living in Columbus exactly one week—one-third of the time before Hetty would come. And she had counted thirty-five white horses, which was more than one-third of a hundred. So it was going to be all right.

On Friday morning she and her mother had breakfast alone, the way they did each day now. Ellen always had the table set before her mother came down. Her mother always fixed something special.

"Ellen," Mrs. Evans said, "do you remember I said I'd give you cooking lessons next summer?"

Ellen nodded. She wished she didn't have to wait so long to learn to cook. She thought she would be the proudest girl in the world the day she made a chocolate cake all by herself. And iced it too.

"Well," Mrs. Evans said, "I've been thinking. I've got

some time now, with the house settled and you taking care of George every morning. So I wondered if you'd like to start cooking lessons this very afternoon."

"Oh, Mother!" Ellen swallowed a piece of toast the wrong way. It made her cough. Her mother patted her on the back.

They were both laughing when she finally stopped.

"May I start with chocolate cake, Mother?" Ellen asked.

Her mother smiled. "I don't see why not," she said.

The cake Ellen made that afternoon didn't rise quite as high as the ones her mother made. But Ellen put the icing on with beautiful curly swoops.

She cut the first piece for her father at supper.

He tasted it. He nodded his head. "No doubt about it," he said. "Excellent flavor! Your mother never did better."

"It's not very high," Ellen said.

"The next one will rise better," her mother promised. "It just takes practice. Would you like to try biscuits for tomorrow's supper?"

Ellen had counted only three horses that day. Her cooking lesson hadn't left much time for sitting on the porch. But her first cake was worth it, she told herself.

The next day she spent most of the afternoon watching,

because biscuits couldn't be started until an hour before supper time. That day she counted six more horses.

But cutting up vegetables for soup on Monday took a long time. So did shredding cheese for macaroni and cheese on Tuesday. Whitey and Bess and Betsy were the only horses she counted those days.

Wednesday morning Mr. Evans said, "Ellen, we finished that cake of yours days ago. Isn't it about time you made another?"

Mrs. Evans looked proud. "Ellen," she said, "that's the finest compliment a cook can receive."

Ellen felt proud too. She said of course she would make another cake. And it turned out higher than the first one, at least on one side. With extra icing on the low half, it looked almost the way Ellen had hoped it would.

The next morning Captain Zollinger won the first four games. In the last one he took six of her checkers in a single move.

"Something bothering you, Ellen?" he asked. "You never let me get away with a trick like that before."

Ellen turned back to the board that stood on an apple box between them. She had been looking up toward Summit Street. Very few wagons came along Stewart Street, where the firehouse stood.

"I'll beat you this last game," she said.

"Poor old Mrs. Ogilvie hasn't been chasing you again, has she?" the captain asked sharply.

"Oh, no," Ellen shook her head. "I always walk straight past her house. I never stare, the way I did that first day."

"But you wave to Mindy every time," the captain said.

Ellen was surprised. She didn't know he had been watching her. "I don't know whether she sees me or not," she said.

"I'm willing to bet she does," the captain said. "I'll bet she watches for you every morning."

"Who moves first?" Ellen asked.

The captain leaned back and folded his arms. "If you ask a fool question like that, there must be something wrong," he said. "You afraid Jim might turn up here again?" he asked suddenly. "And you don't like him?"

"Oh, I do!" Ellen said. "I mean—" She stopped. She knew her face was getting red again.

"Good," the captain said. "I kind of think he likes you too. Asks me every night how many games you won." He rubbed his chin. "I believe you're tired of playing with me, Ellen. That must be why you haven't paid proper attention these last few days."

"It isn't that at all!" Ellen said.

The captain just looked at her.

Ellen took a deep breath. It wasn't fair, she thought, to hurt his feelings in order to keep her secret.

"It's just that I'm counting white horses," she said.

"Counting white horses! Whatever in tarnation for?"

She told him about counting to a hundred, and walking around the block without stopping, and finding something. "And I want to do it before my cousin Hetty moves to Columbus next Thursday," she said.

"I see! I see!" The captain nodded. "Hmm. And Thursday's just a week away. How many you got now?" he asked.

"It was sixty-three last night," Ellen told him. "But with Bess and Betsy this morning again, and the milkman's horse, it's sixty-six now."

"Hmm." The captain thought for a while. "And of

course you don't want to give up your cooking lessons," he said finally. "With your mamma taking all that trouble to teach you—and you getting along so fine."

"No," Ellen said, "I couldn't give them up."

George began to cry.

"All right, George," the captain said. "Your big sister'll take you home. And I'll give your problem some thought, Ellen. I might have an idea by tomorrow. I just might."

The next morning the captain asked right away, "Any luck yesterday, Ellen?"

Ellen could hardly wait to tell him. "Four more!" she said. "First a bakery wagon horse I never saw before. Then the most wonderful thing! Three beautiful white horses like circus horses! They were pulling a red wagon with a calliope in it. Do you suppose there's a circus in town? Do you suppose I might get to see them again?"

"Wouldn't like to say as to that," the captain said. "Still, four is four. You're making progress."

Then he seemed to forget all about white horses.

"Why don't you take a little walk this morning?" he asked, waving down Stewart Street. "I don't know that I feel like checkers today. You can leave George with me," he added.

Ellen couldn't answer him for a moment. She was too

surprised. Then she said stiffly, "All right. But I can take George."

"No, no—just run along. George and I will be peaceful here, just the two of us. With no womenfolks to fuss." The captain closed his eyes as if he were going to take a nap.

Ellen waited a moment. She thought he might open his eyes again and explain that it was all a joke. But he didn't. So she walked away down Stewart Street, her head very high in the air.

She had trusted the captain to have a good idea for her today. Instead he seemed to have forgotten all about her problem. He didn't even want to play checkers with her.

Then she told herself she couldn't blame him for that. She hadn't been a very good partner lately.

She had reached the corner of Poplar Street. On her right, a block away, was her father's new store.

Suddenly Ellen wondered if the captain thought she wanted to visit the store, to see Jim.

"My goodness!" she thought. "The very idea! Is that why he told me to take a walk?"

She marched straight across Poplar Street and on down Stewart. With every step she felt more angry at Captain Zollinger. And more hurt because he would rather take a nap than help her find ways to count white horses.

Halfway to the next corner was a stable door, wide open to the sunshine. Just inside was something bright and red.

Ellen caught her breath. She had recognized it immediately.

"Goot morning!" A fat man with a jolly red face appeared out of nowhere. He had a pail of suds in one hand and a brush in the other. He was getting ready to wash the calliope wagon Ellen had seen the day before.

"Good morning." Ellen's heart was going fast. "I saw your wagon on Summit Street yesterday. With three white horses. They were just beautiful!"

"You would like to see them again, Miss Ellen?" His eyes were twinkling.

"How do you know my name?" Ellen asked.

"Ah-hah! I surprise you, yes?" He laughed. "My friend Captain Zollinger, he say you may come to pay me a visit this morning. He say you like white horses. So you come in please, Miss Ellen, and meet Hans and Fritz and Otto."

Ten minutes later Ellen was back at the firehouse. She threw her arms around the captain and kissed him.

He hadn't been sleeping at all. He had been sitting there talking to George, just waiting for her.

"Oh, thank you!" she said. "Now I can do it! Mr.

Schmid has to take his calliope to the county fair on Sunday. But every other day I'll have six—Whitey and Bess and Betsy, and Otto and Hans and Fritz! So I'll surely get to a hundred by Thursday! And that means I'll be able to walk around the block before Hetty comes!"

Chapter *4* ✻ *One Hundred White Horses*

When Ellen woke up on Thursday the robins were still making their early-morning sounds.

She put on her favorite blue-and-white checked gingham. She was so excited that she buttoned it wrong the first time and had to do it over.

The night before she had counted her ninety-ninth horse. She had only one more to go.

She set the table before the milkman arrived.

As he came up the walk, clattering his basket, she counted Whitey for the last time.

"Lucky, lucky white horse!" she said. "Ding! Ding! Ding!"

She let out her breath with a big sigh after the last Ding!
"One hundred!" she said.

She felt like singing. She felt like dancing.

"Good morning," the milkman said through the open
door.

"Good morning," Ellen said.

She wondered if she should tell him good-by. She
probably wouldn't see him again, she thought. Because if
she didn't have to get up to count Whitey every morning,
she might as well stay in bed the way she used to.

Then a strange thing happened. Suddenly Ellen im-
agined her mother coming downstairs and finding the
table bare.

Ellen knew exactly how her mother would look. Mrs.
Evans' good-morning smile would fade slowly. She might
glance around, wondering if Ellen was hiding to tease
her. Then her face would get a little sad.

"Oh, Mother!" Ellen whispered.

She felt as if she had just waked up after a nightmare.
It was wonderful to know it hadn't really happened.

Ellen knew then that she was going to get up early every
morning, to set the table and have breakfast with her
mother.

And she knew those breakfasts would be even better

from now on because she wouldn't be getting up just for a secret reason of her own.

Ellen shook herself and went to work. She could do a lot of things now besides setting the table. She put bacon in the skillet and broke eggs in a bowl.

"Oh, Ellen, it smells so good!" her mother was saying a few minutes later.

Ellen hugged her harder than usual.

An hour later Mr. Evans was on his way to the store. Mrs. Evans was getting ready to feed George.

"Mother," Ellen said, "would you mind if I take a little walk by myself? Just around the block?"

"Of course not, Ellen," Mrs. Evans said. "It will do you good to have time off from George." She smiled at her over the baby's head. "You look excited, dear. And no wonder—with Hetty coming today."

Ellen swallowed. "Yes," she said. "I won't be long, Mother," she added and went out quickly.

She wondered if her mother would notice the change in her when she came back. She thought it would surely show. The minute she had found something, she was certain she would look different. Because she would feel different.

Ellen didn't hesitate where the Evans' walk joined the

sidewalk. She knew what she wanted to do.

She turned toward Crestview, in the opposite direction from Stewart. That meant she would pass the firehouse after she had already been more than halfway around the block. If she had found something by then, she would show it to the captain. He deserved to be the first one to know.

One step. Two steps. Three steps.

Ellen walked slowly. At each step she looked first at the sidewalk in front of her feet. Then she looked to the left, at the strip of grass between sidewalk and curb. Then she looked to the right, at the edges of people's lawns.

Almost every lawn had a small rise, a foot or two back from the walk. Ellen let herself look to the top of the tiny hills, but no farther. Finding something near a person's house, she had decided, wouldn't really count.

A surprising number of things lay on the sidewalk or in the grass close to it. There were small bits of coal, spilled from ash barrels. There were candy wrappers. There was a bright-red paper cigar band.

She reached the first corner sooner than she had expected. It seemed no time at all before she was turning into Crestview.

There was a grocery store on the street. Someone might

have dropped a penny coming out of the store, she thought.

But no one had.

Near the end of the block, near the corner of Poplar Street, something blue in the grass caught her eye. She bent over it, not breathing. She pushed the grass away.

It was a tiny wheel from a toy train or a toy truck.

Could this be it? Ellen wondered, feeling disappointed. She had told herself she wouldn't care what she found, so long as she found something.

No, she decided. This wasn't really anything at all. It was only a part of a thing.

"I'll know it for sure when I see it," she thought, and straightened up and went on.

In just a minute she was almost at the second corner.

And then she had reached it.

One whole street and half of another—of Summit Street—were already behind her now. But she told herself she wasn't even surprised. She had been sure ahead of time that she wouldn't find what she was looking for on Summit Street. She hadn't really expected to find it on Crestview either.

So everything was all right. Because Poplar Street, the street she had never walked along before, was the street where she most thought it would be.

She took a deep breath and turned the corner.

Poplar seemed to stretch a long distance in front of her. Two blocks away Jim was already at work in her father's store. She wondered if she would ever tell him about counting white horses.

Then she put Jim out of her mind. She didn't want to think about anything but looking—and looking—and looking.

Poplar Street was cleaner than Crestview. There wasn't a single thing on the sidewalk, or near it, until she had walked halfway to Stewart.

Then suddenly she saw a bright fleck of yellow beneath a dandelion leaf. Slowly she stooped down. Her hand was shaking when she lifted the leaf.

The fleck of yellow was a curled-up bit of a broken balloon.

Ellen dropped the leaf quickly and stood up again.

She made her steps smaller. And then smaller still.

Even so, the next corner came closer very fast.

And then she was there. She was standing where Poplar and Stewart met. She had walked more than halfway around the whole block.

And she hadn't found anything.

"But there's all of Stewart yet," Ellen said out loud. "And the rest of Summit Street. Why did I ever think it would be on Poplar anyway?"

She turned into Stewart. One step. And another. And another.

She came to the place where the sidewalk widened, where it stretched smooth and clean right up to the firehouse.

She had been so sure she would have something to show the captain by the time she got here. Now she didn't even want to see him.

She didn't look up toward his chair until the last possible moment.

He wasn't there. The chair was empty.

At first she was relieved. Then she was puzzled. Then she remembered.

It was still very early. This was the hour when he polished the engine every morning.

Without calling to him, she went quickly past the open doorway.

Beyond the firehouse she slowed down again. At each step she looked first at the sidewalk around her feet. After that she looked to the left. After that she looked to the right. Then she took the next step.

She came to the fence around Mrs. Ogilvie's house.

A crumpled sheet of newspaper had blown against it.
And a candy wrapper. And a paper milk-bottle cap. And
more newspaper.

"Little girl! Please! Wait a moment!"

It was Mrs. Ogilvie. She was coming down her porch
steps.

"Me?" Ellen asked.

"Yes, please." Mrs. Ogilvie was hurrying along the
walk to the gate.

Quickly Ellen picked up her left foot so that she was standing on just the right one. That way she wasn't breaking the rule. She wasn't really stopping. She was just taking a very slow step.

"Oh, dear!" she thought. "Can't she see I'm going somewhere?"

She remembered thinking how frightened she would be if Mrs. Ogilvie ever spoke to her again. So she supposed she must be feeling frightened now.

"I wanted to ask a favor of you," Mrs. Ogilvie was saying as she reached the gate. "I wanted to ask if you would come in for a moment and meet my granddaughter."

"Oh, no, ma'am!" Ellen said. "I couldn't!" She remembered to be polite. "I mean, I just can't stop now. I'm sorry, ma'am."

"I see." Mrs. Ogilvie looked at her. She didn't really seem like an ogre at all. Her face wasn't even angry, the way it had been that day at the window. It was only very sad.

"You don't wish to come in because I once told you to go away," Mrs. Ogilvie said. "I think I could explain that to you," she added. "But perhaps you wouldn't understand."

"Oh, I do understand," Ellen said quickly. She was still

on one foot. It was getting hard to keep her balance. "Captain Zollinger told me how people came on the trolleys and all. But I wasn't really staring that day. Anyway, I didn't mean to. Only when I thought she waved to me—"

"She did wave to you," Mrs. Ogilvie said. "And she has watched for your wave every morning since. That's what made me realize how lonely she is. That's why I hoped you would come in and talk to her for a while."

Ellen clenched her hands tight behind her back. "I'm awfully sorry," she said. "But, you see, I'm walking around the block."

The moment the words were out she knew how strange

they must sound. Mrs. Ogilvie would think she was just inventing an excuse not to meet Mindy. And Mindy would think the same thing when her grandmother told her what Ellen had said.

"It's not," Ellen said quickly, "that I'm just plain walking around the block. I have to, you see. To look for something."

"Oh, I'm sorry, child." Mrs. Ogilvie smiled. She had a very nice smile. But even when she smiled, her face was still sad. "Something you lost?"

"Oh, dear!" Ellen thought unhappily. Mrs. Ogilvie's question made her think of what Mrs. Ogilvie had lost. And of what Mindy had lost too.

"No." Ellen shook her head. The toe of her left foot touched the ground, but she didn't even know it. "Something that—well, something I thought maybe I would find."

At that moment she would have given anything she owned to be strong and sure like Hetty. Hetty always knew what she wanted to do, and she did it. She finished what she started. She wouldn't let any old woman change her mind for her just because the old woman looked sad even when she smiled.

But Ellen's mind was always being changed by things

like that. It was being changed right now. And she couldn't help it. She couldn't stop it happening.

It had already happened.

She wasn't going to finish her walk straight around the block. Even if she had waited three weeks to do it. Even if she had counted a hundred white horses. Even if she had promised herself that when she found something— and she had been so sure she would—her whole life would be changed.

Now, she supposed, her life wouldn't ever be changed. She would go on being Hetty's shadow forever.

Because she couldn't refuse Mrs. Ogilvie. She just couldn't.

"I don't really have to look for it," Ellen said. "I can come in if you want me to." She tried hard to smile. People who accepted invitations were supposed to smile.

"I'm so glad, my dear!" Mrs. Ogilvie looked almost happy.

There were squares of colored glass in the top half of the big front door. There were squares of black and white marble on the floor of the hall. The stairway at the far end of the hall went round and round, up and up.

"Mindy's room is in the tower," Mrs. Ogilvie said. "But I guess you know that."

Ellen nodded, following her upward. "Yes, ma'am."

"Here we are." Mrs. Ogilvie stopped beside an open door.

Beyond it was the most wonderful room Ellen had ever seen. It was round, with tall windows. A window seat ran around the room beneath them. Mindy was sitting on the window seat. She got up.

She was about Ellen's size, with hair almost the same color.

"This is my granddaughter, Mindy," Mrs. Ogilvie said. "Mindy, dear, this is the girl—"

"I know," Mindy said quickly. "Hello."

"Hello," Ellen said. "I'm Ellen Evans."

"I always wondered what your name was," Mindy said. Mrs. Ogilvie went away.

Hetty would know what to say at a time like this, Ellen thought. She looked around the room. "It's wonderful up here," she said.

"Yes," Mindy said. "When we used to visit here, my sister and I—" She stopped. Then she started again. "Did you lose something down there on the sidewalk? I was watching you. I thought—maybe I could help you find it."

"It wasn't anything I lost," Ellen said. "It was only—

well, something I was supposed to find because of the white horses."

The words had come out by themselves.

"White horses?" Mindy smiled for the first time. "What white horses?"

And so, because she didn't know what else to do, Ellen told her about moving day and Aunt Jo. And about Whitey and Bess and Betsy.

They were sitting on the window seat by then.

She told about George too. And about Captain Zollinger and the checker games. And Jim of course. And the cooking lessons. And the captain's friend who had the calliope, and Otto and Hans and Fritz.

"So I got to a hundred this morning," Ellen said. "And I was walking around the block—"

She stopped. She had meant to leave that part out.

"Oh, Ellen!" Mindy said. "And you hadn't found anything yet when Grandma brought you in here! So it's my fault you—"

"It doesn't matter," Ellen said. Because Mindy looked so sorry. And because since it couldn't work now anyway, she might as well pretend she didn't care.

"But it does!" Mindy said. "If only I hadn't told Grandma about wishing I knew you! Then she wouldn't

have stopped you."

"But I'm glad she did," Ellen said.

And suddenly, after she had said it, she knew it was really true.

"Really," she added.

Mindy looked her straight in the eyes.

Ellen looked back.

They both smiled a little. They went on smiling.

"If you want to take cooking lessons with me," Ellen said suddenly, "I'm sure Mother would let you. If your grandmother would."

"I'm almost sure she would!" Mindy said. "Especially if we both asked her together. And maybe I could help you with George sometimes."

"And we could both play checkers with the captain," Ellen said. "Taking turns."

"And couldn't we count white horses, Ellen?" Mindy said. "If you didn't mind starting over? If you wanted to."

"I think it would be wonderful doing it together!" Ellen said. "And I guess we could tell Hetty about them too."

"Hetty?" Mindy asked.

"You know. My cousin," Ellen said. Then she realized that Mindy didn't know. Ellen hadn't mentioned Hetty yet. She had forgotten all about her!

"Hetty's family is moving to Columbus today," Ellen said, "into the other half of our house. She's pretty bossy. But if we don't want to do what she says, we'll just tell her No."

Suddenly Ellen began to giggle. "My goodness!" she said. "I never thought of that before! I guess I could have said No to her a million times. Only I was afraid."

"Oh, Ellen!" Mindy said. "I'm sure you were never afraid of anything."

"Well, I was," Ellen said. "But I'm not anymore. I don't know why, but all of a sudden I'm not."

And then she did know.

"My goodness!" she said. "Of course! Because I found something!"

"You found something walking around the block?" Mindy asked. She looked astonished but happy. "That's wonderful! Why didn't you tell me before?"

"Why, because I didn't even know at first that you— that we— And just imagine!" Ellen said. "I used to think it couldn't possibly be anything even as good as a ring or a pin or a locket!"

"And it's something better? Please!" Mindy said. "Tell me!"

"Oh!" Ellen said. She thought she had. She thought Mindy had understood what she meant.

"Well—" Some things were hard to say out loud.

"Of course," Ellen began again, "I guess I would have found you some way. Or Hetty would have. But this way is so special! And when you think that if I hadn't taken George for a walk that first day—"

"Oh, Ellen!" Mindy said. "Just suppose you hadn't!"

Then suddenly Mindy sucked in her breath. "Oh, Ellen!" she said again. "Do you mean you found *me*?"

Ellen nodded.

She and Mindy looked at each other. They each took a big breath at the same moment. They held it. Then they let it out. And they were sort of laughing. And sort of hugging each other.

Ellen knew she would remember this moment forever, because it was the happiest moment of her life.

"I have a friend!" she thought. "And I found her all by myself!"

"Lucky, lucky white horse!" Mindy was saying. "It must be the most powerful magic in the world. Don't you think so?"

"Oh, yes!" Ellen said. "In the whole, whole world!"

Format by Robin Sherwood
Set in Linotype Electra
Composed and bound by American Book–Stratford Press
Printed by The Murray Printing Company
HARPER & ROW, PUBLISHERS, INCORPORATED

MAR   1972